Tick Tock Tales

Margaret K. McElderry Books
Macmillan Publishing Company
866 Third Avenue
New York, NY 10022

Macmillan Publishing Company is part of the Maxwell Communication
Group of Companies.

Text copyright © 1993 by Margaret Mahy
Illustrations copyright © 1993 by Wendy Smith
First published by Orion Children's Books, London

Printed in Italy
2   4   6   8   10   9   7   5   3   1
ISBN 0-689-50604-X

MARGARET MAHY

Tick Tock Tales

Stories to read around the clock

Illustrated by

Wendy Smith

MARGARET K. McELDERRY BOOKS
New York
Maxwell Macmillan International
New York   Oxford   Singapore   Sydney

Contents

Contents

POODLUM HOODLUM

Sandwich Street was a street full of pets. There was Wuffy on the corner, and Scruffy by the shop. Cats sunned themselves at kitchen doors. Canaries sang in cages.

"I need a pet, too. Let's get a dog," Caspar begged his mother.

"Play with the dog next door," she suggested.

"But that dog isn't a real dog! It's a pompom-poodlum," cried Caspar. "Pompom-poodlums can't play."

The pompom-poodlum belonged to Mrs. Montague-Montague. She had had his black poodle-wool clipped into pompoms – a pompom tied with a blue ribbon on top of his head, and two pompoms, both with blue ribbons, on his tail.

"I won't play tricks . . . I won't throw sticks for a silly old pompom-poodlum!" cried Caspar. "If I have a dog, I want it to be a hum-hum-hoodlum."

The pompom-poodlum sat on the other side of the fence and sighed.

I wish someone would throw sticks for me, he thought. If I ever have a boy, I would like a boy like Caspar.

"Pumfrey!" called Mrs. Montague-Montague, for that is what she called her pompom-poodlum. "We're moving to the city. What fun we'll have: gallivanting to galas and garden parties – me in my new pink dress, and you in new pink bows. Soon we'll be well away from Sandwich Street, with Wuffy on the corner and Scruffy by the shop, and the noisy, nosy Caspar next door."

The pompom-poodlum was packed into a traveling cage with a flowery carpet and a pink cushion. The man in charge of the move slid the cage into the back of the van. The van set off for the city.

The pompom-poodlum whined and sighed in the back of the van. With his clever paws and pointed nose he wiggled and jiggled the catch on the back of his cage.

The van stopped in a distant town. The driver opened the back of the van to check the furniture. Out shot the pompom-poodlum. Off he went, pompoms and all, around the corner, past a lamppost, under a fence, across two gardens, and through a hedge, leaving a trail of blue ribbons behind him. At last he hid deep down in a dark, damp, dirty ditch. No one looked for him there.

Night fell. The moon came out, and so did the pompom-poodlum. There was no van. There was no kennel. Where was a pompom-poodlum to go?

He hid in gardens, where his pompoms looked like neatly clipped bushes. He sneaked through shadows. And no one saw him because he was shadow-colored. He ate dinner from the dishes of other dogs.

I must find my way to Sandwich Street, the pompom-poodlum thought to himself.

Cold winds blew on him, but he curled up and put his pompom tail over his nose. New black wool began busily growing all over his bare patches.

Creeping through gardens, and diving along ditches, night after night, day after day, the pompom-poodlum wove his way back toward Sandwich Street.

Nobody threw sticks for him, but a few people threw stones at him. Once, a dogcatcher nearly found him in a park, but the pompom-poodlum pretended to be a statue of black stone, and the dogcatcher walked past without noticing him. Once, a laborer laughed at him, and then tossed him a sandwich. Sandwich Street! thought the pompom-poodlum, as he wolfed it down. I'm going in the right direction.

The pompom-poodlum robbed trash cans – he was amazed to see what people tossed into them! He raided trash dumps on the edges of towns and saw even more astonishing things. Then, off and away he went, still searching for Sandwich Street, growing wilder and woollier as he went. Black wool grew down over his paws. His bright brown eyes blinked through a curling fringe. There was nobody to clip, comb, or care for him anymore.

Late one evening, the pompom-poodlum limped around a corner. Suddenly, there it was, exactly as he remembered it – Sandwich Street – with Wuffy on the corner, and Scruffy by the shop, and kitchens full of cats, and cages of canaries.

"Mommy, look! There's a funny sort of sheep lolloping along out there," cried Caspar.

"That's not a sheep. Its legs are too long, and I can see a pointed nose in all that wool. Besides, it's not lolloping. It's limping," said his mother. "Poor thing!"

"It could sleep in our shed," suggested Caspar cunningly.

"Well, all right," said his mother. "Just for tonight."

The pompom-poodlum sat up and begged, waving his sore front paws in front of him.

"Oh, Mom, do let him come inside and lie down by the fire," said Caspar, begging, too, and waving his hands.

"You said you didn't want a pompom-poodlum," cried his mother.

"But this dog's wild. This dog's woolly. It isn't a pompom-poodlum. It's a hum-hum-hoodlum!" cried Caspar. "That's exactly the sort of dog I've always wanted."

And Caspar gave the hum-hum-hoodlum a quick hug. The hum-hum-hoodlum licked his ear.

"He likes me," said Caspar. "He can stay, can't he, Mom?"

"We'll see," she replied.

" 'We'll see' means 'yes,' doesn't it?" he asked.

"It might," she said.

" 'It might' really means 'yes,' doesn't it? Go on. Say it! Please, Mom, say 'yes'! I promise I'll feed him. I promise I'll throw sticks for him and play tricks for him. Do say 'yes'! "

"Oh, yes, then. Yes, yes, yes, yes, yes!" cried Caspar's mother, and hugged him. "Are you happy now?"

"Oh, yes, yes, yes, yes, yes!" yelled Caspar.

Caspar and the hum-hum-hoodlum were both enormously happy.

In the distant city, Mrs. Montague-Montague bought herself two new little dogs. She tied pink ribbons around their topknots so that they matched her pink dress when they gallivanted together at garden parties.

Back in Sandwich Street, the hum-hum-hoodlum-pompom-poodlum had his fringe clipped back from over his eyes, but he never ever wore pompoms or ribbons again. And he and his friend Caspar played tricks and chased sticks happily ever after.

THE BIRD CHILD

A certain small girl once lived in a big city that had a forest on its northern edge and an orphanage on its southern edge. The little girl was an orphan. She had no father or mother, only an aunt. But this aunt was of the forgetful kind. One day, when they were having a picnic in the forest, the aunt forgot she had a little girl to look after. She wandered off home, packed her suitcase, and went to South America. She was never heard of again.

The little girl waited and waited for her to come back. Fortunately the aunt had left her under a wild apple tree. She lay on her back watching the pattern of blue sky, green leaves, and red apples. When the apples fell, she ate them. On the third day of waiting, two pigeons flew down and looked at the little girl very hard.

"Are you going to live here forever?" they asked her, but the little girl was too small to explain that she had been left there by her aunt.

"My dear," said the father pigeon to the mother pigeon, "I think she has been left behind by some picnickers. They are always leaving eggshells and banana peels around. Now they have left a child."

"It is very untidy of them," said the mother pigeon. "Poor little girl! Shall we adopt her?"

Now, in this forest lived all the different kinds of birds in the world, and the pigeons called them all together. They began to make a special nest for the little girl. First of all they wove tree twigs together to make a floor and walls. Then the thrushes and blackbirds lined it with straw and mud to keep out the wind and rain. Then the sparrows, finches, and warblers lined it with moss and feathers for softness.

Working together, some of the strongest birds lifted the little girl into the nest. They brought her blackberries and grass seed to eat, and even a few worms. She just opened her mouth and they poked food into it.

It was much easier than living with the aunt who used to say, "Sit up straight and don't make a lot of crumbs when you eat."

As the weeks went by, the birds grew very fond of the little girl and were always trying to think of ways to amuse her.

Because she hated to see them fly away and leave her, they made her a pair of wings out of twigs and tree gum, and feathers. The little girl soon learned to use them cleverly. She flew with the birds in the sunshine. She soared and twisted in and out of the forest trees, chasing the birds and gathering her own blackberries and seeds. Living like this she grew strong and brown and wild. Her hair was tangly, all full of leaves and flowers. Her clothes got torn to pieces and fell off, but this made it much simpler when she wanted to go swimming.

Every few months the birds made her a new pair of wings, brighter and stronger than those she had outgrown.

One day, a hunter, hunting around, saw a flash of blue in the green trees. Flying on wings made by peacocks and kingfishers, the little girl spun into sight for a moment and then was lost again. The hunter did not know that the birds had made wings for her.

He thought she had grown them all on her own. He went and brought back another hunter and a circus owner. They set up a table in the middle of the forest with a birthday cake on it. Before long the Bird Child came down to look at it, and then the hunters threw nets over her. Her great wings broke and crumpled.

The hunters and the circus owner were very angry when they found her wings were just tied on with ribbons woven of grass, but there was nothing they could do about it. So the hunters took the little girl out of the forest, right across the city to the orphanage. It was a square brown building in a square brown yard. The woman in charge was Mrs. Parsley. She did not enjoy her job very much. She really wanted to spend her time growing tomatoes and strawberries. Instead, she had to look after thirty lively, grubby children. When the hunters gave her the Bird Child she was not pleased.

"Tisk! Tisk!" she went with her tongue and took the Bird Child inside. She scrubbed her and rubbed her but she could not make her pale like the other orphans. She could not brush her tangly hair either, so she snipped it off. She dressed the Bird Child in a brown dress and put shoes on her feet, so that she could not run. The walls around the orphanage were as tall as trees and there was a lock on the gate.

The little Bird Child grew thinner and quieter. She became paler than any of the other orphans. Mrs. Parsley gave her cod-liver oil, but it did not make her better. (Mrs. Parsley should have given her a beakful of honey or a few seeds. But Mrs. Parsley did not think of that.)

Once a week the mayor of the city used to come and count the orphans. He was very proud of his neat, well-run orphanage.

"Where did the new orphan come from?" asked the mayor. "She doesn't look to be a very good one."

"Some hunters found her in the forest," said Mrs. Parsley. "You never know *where* orphans are going to turn up these days."

Just then the mayor and Mrs. Parsley heard a noise like the wind, though there was no wind. They looked up at the hills on the other side of the city and saw a cloud rise from the secret heart of the forest. It swirled and eddied like smoke, but it was not smoke. It shimmered and shivered like silk, but it was not silk. Mrs. Parsley and the mayor stared uneasily. The cloud came closer.

"It's birds!" said Mrs. Parsley, amazed.
"Birds!" cried the mayor like an echo.
Sparrows, thrushes, blackbirds,
peacocks, pigeons, parrots and
pelicans, firebirds, pheasants and
flamingos, swans and sea gulls, egrets and
eagles, herons, hummingbirds, and various finches
all were flying straight toward the orphanage, making
the air whisper and the leaves stir and rustle with
the wind of their wings.

"Well, I've never seen so many birds!" said Mrs.
Parsley suspiciously. "It's not natural. They'll drop
feathers all over the orphanage lawn. And it has just
been rolled and raked."

Down in the orphanage yard, one orphan looked up at
the birds and cried out to them in a voice that was
curious and lonely. She held her arms out as if she might
fly up and join them. The cloud of birds wheeled and
swept down, making a great storm. For a moment the
mayor and Mrs. Parsley could see nothing but bright
whirling feathers. Then the birds rose again and flew off
toward the forest. They took all the orphans with them.

Mrs. Parsley and the mayor stared after them. "Those birds have taken the city's orphans!" cried the mayor. "And they haven't filled in any adoption forms."

The birds flew back to the forest. They had come to the orphanage looking for their Bird Child, but, because they could not tell one orphan from another, they had taken the lot. They carried all the orphans into the green shade of the forest, and began looking after them. First they built them nests, then they fed them with honey. The orphans sat in a row and the birds dropped honey into their open mouths. Then the birds made the orphans wings. All the orphans became Bird Children.

Mrs. Parsley spent all that spring with a spade digging up the orphanage lawn. She grew the most remarkable tomatoes. On summer evenings she would look up from her garden to see the Bird Children, tossing like bright kites over the green roof of the forest, their wings, wide and shining, carrying them up toward the stars.

THE ADVENTURES OF LITTLE MOUSE

Once a mouse family lived under the floor of a playroom. There was a mother mouse and a father mouse. There was a big sister mouse, called Mousikin, and a baby brother mouse, called Little Mouse.

They had a pleasant mousehole with two doors. One door opened into a toy cupboard in the playroom. The other opened into a long hall. Mother and Father Mouse ran down the long hall at night. They searched for crumbs, or went into the kitchen to steal cheese. Mousikin and Little Mouse were not allowed to run in the hall. However, Mousikin was sometimes allowed to go into the toy cupboard. Little Mouse was too small to go anywhere. How he longed to see the world outside!

"What is the world like, Mousikin?" he would ask. "Is it strange? Is it exciting? What smells are there in the world, Mousikin?"

"It is very strange out in the world, Little Mouse," said Mousikin. "The world is a lot of shelves one on top of the other. On the shelves are soft, staring creatures with round eyes. They do not blink or wink or even see anything. They don't smile or twitch their whiskers. They just sit there. They are called toys. There is a striped box, and if you open that box out leaps a little striped man – bang! And he grins at you. He is called Jack-in-the-box. There is a round red ball that would roll and bounce if there was room. There are blocks too. You can make mouse castles with them. The world smells of dust and rubber and books."

"What are books, Mousikin?"

"Books are all sizes and colors, Little Mouse. You turn the pages. You look at the pictures. You grow wise and clever."

"What does it mean to be wise, Mousikin?"

"It means to know all sorts of things, Little Mouse. It means to know why cheese smells so nice, and how to tie a bell around the neck of a cat. It means to know how to bake bread or sing a song, or to know where sugar comes from."

"Is it good to be wise, Mousikin?"

"It is the best thing in the world, Little Mouse. That is why I am teaching myself to read. I can read 'A is for Apple, B is for Bear.' I can read long words too."

Little Mouse thought for a moment.

"Will you tell me the new words you learn, Mousikin? Then I will be wise, too. I will be the wisest Little Mouse in the world."

So Mousikin would come back from the toy cupboard and tell Little Mouse the new words she had learned. Little Mouse learned 'A is for Apple, B is for Bear,' too. He liked the long words best.

"What long words Little Mouse is saying now!" said Father Mouse proudly.

Then one day Mousikin came back from the toy cupboard, her black eyes round and shining.

"Oh, Little Mouse! Do you know what I saw today in the toy cupboard? I saw a picture in a book, Little Mouse. It was a picture of a huge monster, bigger than a cat, bigger than a dog . . . bigger even than a rocking horse. Its name was the longest in the world. Its name – listen carefully, Little Mouse – its name was Brontosaurus."

Little Mouse twitched his whiskers.

"Brontosaurus!" he said. "That word is longer than I am."

"It means Thunder Lizard, Little Mouse. This monster was so big it was called the Thunder Lizard. It had a long, long neck and a teeny-tiny head. It had a great fat body and stumpy legs. Behind it was a tail as long as its neck."

"Was its tail longer than my tail, Mousikin?" asked Little Mouse, who thought he had a very long tail indeed.

"Of course it was, you foolish Little Mouse. Its tail was longer than yours, longer than mine. It was longer than a piece of string. It was the tail of a monster."

Little Mouse dreamed of the monster called Brontosaurus. He said its name over and over to himself. For two whole days he did not think of anything else but the brontosaurus. He thought of its long neck and its teeny-tiny head. He thought of its tail.

"Brontosaurus means Thunder Lizard," said Little Mouse to himself. He began to think of seeing the picture of the brontosaurus for himself. "I would like to see the picture of that brontosaurus."

Little Mouse asked to go to the toy cupboard with Mousikin.

"No, no, Little Mouse!" said his mother. "You are too small."

"If someone opened the cupboard door you would not know where to run to," said Father Mouse. "Children would catch you and put you in a cage. When you are older you can go with Mousikin."

Little Mouse said nothing. He was making a special Little Mouse plan to go on his own, when no one was looking.

Next day, when his parents were away and Mousikin was asleep, Little Mouse stole out on his own. He wanted to get to the toy cupboard but he did not know the way. Down a dark passage he went, his whiskers prickling with excitement. He did not know where he was going. It was not the passage to the toy cupboard – it was the passage to the hall.

As he went Little Mouse heard a roar like thunder. Could it be a brontosaurus roaring somewhere? He listened carefully. Then he went on very slowly. He came to the mousehole and peeped out. The mousehole was behind a big black chest in the hall. No one could see Little Mouse, but Little Mouse could see everything that was going on. The first thing he saw was a brontosaurus.

Little Mouse knew it was a brontosaurus because it had a long, snaky neck and teeny-tiny head. It had a long tail too – a long, long tail. It was the longest tail Little Mouse had ever seen.

Someone was taking the brontosaurus for a walk. Little Mouse could see a pair of feet walking beside it and a hand on its shiny neck. Its teeny-tiny head was flat on the ground. As it went by it roared like thunder and sucked up the dust.

"The brontosaurus is a Thunder Lizard," whispered Little Mouse softly. The whole world shook as the brontosaurus went by.

Down at the end of the hall a door opened. Someone called out, "Will you be much longer?"

"No," said the owner of the feet that were taking the brontosaurus for a walk. "I will just put the vacuum cleaner away." Someone picked up the brontosaurus, and unplugged its tail from the wall. Someone carried the brontosaurus away.

Little Mouse scurried back home down the mouse passage. How surprised his parents and Mousikin would be to hear how brave he had been!

"Mousikin, Mousikin! I have seen a real one. It is bigger than we ever thought and it really roars like thunder. Not only that, Mousikin, it eats dirt and dust for its supper. I saw it, Mousikin – and, Mousikin, it had another name. It is called Vacuum Cleaner."

"Oh, Little Mouse!" said Mousikin. "How wise you are now."

"Yes," said Father Mouse, "but he should not have run away like that. Tomorrow you can go to the toy cupboard with Mousikin, but you must never go to the hall again. The brontosaurus might get you next time."

Little Mouse twitched his whiskers.

"Are you pleased, Little Mouse? Are you happy?" asked Mousikin.

Little Mouse smiled a mouse smile.

"I am so happy, I feel as if all the world were made of cheese," he said.

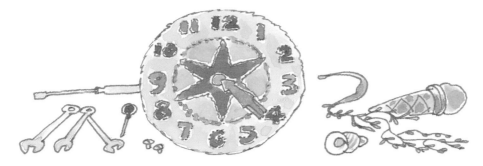

THE BOY WHO MADE THINGS UP

There was once a father who had a little boy. However, it was a bit of a waste for this father to have a boy, really, because he was much too interested in his work. He worked all through the week and then, on the weekends, he spent all his time under the car fixing it so that he could take it to work again the next week. You will understand he did not have much time to spend with his little boy. In fact, all the little boy ever saw of his father was a pair of boots sticking out from under the car. This was not much fun. With no father to tell him exciting stories, the boy had to make up his own stories. He became very good at making things up.

Well, one day his father's car broke down a long way from home and had to be taken away to a garage, and there was not much for him to do on the weekend. He felt strange and unprotected with no car to crawl under. The space of hills and sky made him feel nervous. However, he decided to make the best of it, and take his boy for a walk instead.

"Come on, Michael," he called. "We'll wander down to the crossroads, shall we?"

Michael was delighted to go for a walk with his father. He marched cheerfully along beside him, looking at him curiously. He wasn't used to seeing all of his father at the same time.

After a while he said, "Shall we just walk along, Dad, or shall we make some of it up?"

"Make some of it up?" said his puzzled father. "Make what up? . . . Oh well, whatever *you* like, Michael," he added in a kind voice.

"Shall we go by *that* path then?" said the little boy, pointing. Over the field ran a path that his father did not recognize. It was narrow, and a bit tangled, with foxgloves leaning over it, and bright stones poking through the ground.

"That's funny!" said his father. "I've never seen that path before. There's no doubt you miss a lot by driving everywhere. Where does this path go?"

"It goes to the sea," said Michael, leading the way, brushing the dew off the foxgloves.

"But the sea is fifty miles away," cried his father. "It can't lead to the sea."

"We're making it up, remember," said Michael.

"Oh, just pretending," his father replied, as if he understood everything.

"The sea is on the other side of that little hill," Michael went on, and his father was amazed to see the path hump itself into a little hill in front of them. At the same time a soft murmuring filled the air, as if giants were breathing quietly in their sleep. Michael and his father hurried up the little hill. There on the other side was the sea. The sand stretched a long way, starred with shells, striped with seaweed. There was no one else on all that long, sunny shore. There weren't even any sea gulls – just the sand, with the sea dancing along its edge.

"I told you. I told you," yelled Michael, and charged onto the beach. His father followed him, frowning with amazement.

"If I'd known we were coming here," he said, trying hard to make his voice sound ordinary, "I'd have brought buckets and spades."

"There are buckets and spades over by that log," Michael told him. "And our bathing trunks! Mine are wrapped up in a blue towel. What about yours?"

"Er . . ." said his father.

"Just make it up," Michael cried. "I'll make it up for you. An orange-striped towel, almost new."

The log lay, half in, half out of the sand , as if it was trying to burrow down and get away from the sun. There were the buckets and spades. There were the bathing trunks and towels.

"Swim first!" decided Michael.

"It's a bit coldish. Let's make it a warm day."

Immediately the wind died down and the sunshine grew hotter. Michael's father stood frowning at his orange-striped towel, almost new.

"I'm ready," Michael said, dancing before him. "You're slow, Dad. Last one in is nothing but a sand flea." He raced, running and jumping, into the waves. His sand flea father followed.

"Be careful!" he shouted. "Remember you can't swim, and I haven't done much swimming myself for a few years."

"Say you're a wonderful swimmer!" suggested Michael. "Say we can both swim to the islands."

"The islands?" said his father. Sure enough, out on the horizon were islands scattered like seeds in the furrows of the sea.

The boy and his father swam out to the islands without getting in the least bit tired. The water was warm, yet tingling, and as clear as green glass. Shoals of bright fish, as small and shiny as needles, followed them and tickled their feet.

Down, down, far down under the water, the sand shone silver with black fish all over it, like a night sky pulled inside out. The boy and his father swam in and out among the islands. Waves burst on the rocks around them and rainbows in the spray curled over their heads. Sometimes they swam facedown and peered through the clear water, watching fish and sand.

"I could swim all day," his father cried.

"But we've got to get back for our ice cream," declared Michael.

So they swam lazily back to the long, empty beach, still quiet except for the sighing, breathing sea.

"Here! Where will we get any ice cream?" asked his father, frowning again. "There are no shops."

"Can't you understand how things work yet?" Michael cried despairingly. "We make something up! Look!"

Far down the beach something was moving closer and closer. It was a tall, thin man dressed in black and white squares, like a harlequin or a chess board. He was holding a blue frilly sunshade over his head with one hand and carrying a basket in the other. With his feet he furiously pedaled a yellow bicycle. As he passed them he put the basket into Michael's hands.

Then he turned his bicycle and rode straight into the sea. For a few minutes his blue sunshade bobbed above the water and then a green wave curled slowly over it, like a curtain coming down at a theater. They couldn't see him anymore. "See what I mean?" asked Michael. "Much better than a shop."

The basket was full of ice cream with nuts in it, and strawberries on top. Michael's father looked grown-up and thoughtful. After they had eaten the ice cream, they played with their buckets and spades for a while, and then they decided it was time to go back down the foxglove path. All the way home his father looked more and more thoughtful and grown-up. Every time he looked at Michael he blinked.

As soon as they got home, Michael was sent to wash his hands – a thing that usually happens to boys. His father stood beside his mother, drying the dishes she was washing.

"Tell me, my dear," he said, in a quiet, nervous voice. "Does Michael often make things up?"

"Oh yes!" said Michael's mother. "He's rather a lonely little boy and he's always making up some adventure. He's very good at it."

"But," said his father in a very astonished voice, "he took me to the *beach*. We went *swimming*. I got *sunburned*. My shoes are full of *sand*. And yet I *know* the sea is fifty miles away."

"Oh yes," said Michael's mother very casually, "I told you. He's very good at making things up. I've told you before, but you were too busy listening to the car."

"It's very strange – very strange," said his father.

"But lots of fun!" his mother added.

"Yes, I suppose it is," said his father. He thought some more.

"I don't think I'll spend so much time with the car from now on. Michael needs the guidance of a father. A father and son should see a lot of each other, don't you think?" he asked.

"Oh yes, I'm sure they should," said Michael's mother, and she smiled a smile that was almost a grin at the saucer she was washing.

SAILOR JACK AND THE TWENTY ORPHANS

There was once a boy called Tom who was an orphan and who lived with nineteen other orphans in a big house called Bartholomew's Institution. They had no fathers, only a board of governors.

And there was once a sailor called Jack, who had sailed all around the seven seas seven times. Tom and Jack met on a wharf where they liked to sit, dangling their legs over the edge. Tom loved listening to stories and Jack loved telling them, so they got on very well.

The story Tom liked best was when Jack told how he had fought the terrible giant oyster, and how he had been captured by the monkey king.

Tom listened as if he had ten ears to keep busy, instead of only two.

All the time Jack was talking the tide came up and up, trying to get at their dangling feet, and they did not even notice it.

Then Tom explained that he was one of twenty boy orphans who loved sea stories, and he told Jack all about Bartholomew's Institution. Jack listened, amazed.

"It sounds a poor life to me," he said at last. "I'll tell you what! I've always had a fancy to adopt some boys to be my sons and listen to my stories. Now it seems to me that twenty is a good, satisfying number. I'll save up my money, and, this time next year, I'll come back and adopt you all. How's *that* for an idea?"

"It's a splendid idea!" Tom cried. "The best you ever had! I will meet you here in a year's time and I'll bring the other orphans too. Then you can adopt us, and we'll all go to sea together."

Hardly had they settled this when the tide slopped into their shoes, so that they knew it was time to say good-bye. They shook hands and each went his way, after promising once more to meet there in a year's time.

Well, how does a poor sailor like Jack get enough money to adopt twenty orphans? He becomes a dashing pirate! This is what Jack did. He joined one of the wildest crews that ever flew the Jolly Roger.

Unfortunately, though he got on well with his saving of money, he got on badly with the pirates. They were a slouching, grubby lot, and, though they were brave and bold at fighting with swords, the thought of soap and water made them turn as pale as cheese. (Jack, of course, was smart and polite and washed at least once a day.)

Then, too, the pirates spent all their money in a wasteful and reckless fashion, whereas Jack saved his, hoping to get enough to adopt his twenty orphans.

One day the pirate captain up and said to Jack:

"Jack, you son-of-a-sea-cook, it seems to me your heart isn't in your work. Why don't you spend your money in wild and riotous living like a pirate should, instead of hoarding it, like a magpie or a landlubber, in that suitcase under your bunk?"

"Well, I'm saving it for this and that,"
said Jack. "Notably because I have it in mind
to adopt twenty orphan boys to be my sons."

The pirate captain's mouth fell open, and he
was so put about with surprise that he could not speak.

"Jack!" he cried at last. "You'll never make a pirate!
Orphans indeed! Where's your knavery and wicked-
ness? Jack," he roared, "we'll have to maroon you!
No one is more sorry than myself, but there you are – it's
one of the pirate rules."

"I'm always willing to keep the rules, Captain," said
Jack smartly, "no matter how much discomfort it may
mean to me personally."

Marooning means that a sailor is left alone on an
island with nothing but his clothes, some salt pork, and a
box of matches. On the first island they came to the
pirates marooned Jack, taking his share of the treasure
away with them. He was left alone on the strangest little
island in the world.

It was strange because it was a long and pointed little
island and because it had one tall palm tree on it. And it
was strange because, although it had only one palm tree,
it had fifty monkeys who leaped and chattered at Jack
and followed him everywhere he went.

Lastly it was strange because on the top of the palm tree perched an old poll parrot with a telescope under its wing, which isn't a thing you'd find on most islands.

"Well," said Jack. "I've sailed the seven seas seven times, but never have I seen such an island."

Night fell, and it was cold – so cold that Jack felt his bones were turning to ice. How does a freezing sailor warm himself up? He dances hornpipes up and down the beach and sings a sea chantey. This is what Jack did. Faster and faster he danced and, as he did so, he thought he felt the island rock beneath him though he was as light of foot and as nimble as a sea cook's cat.

Now that's odd, Jack thought, islands shouldn't rock as easily as that.

As he thought this thought, he was surprised to hear a deep voice call . . .

"Who is that whose heel and toe
Make my island rocking go?"
Jack answered quickly and grammatically.
"It is I, good sailor John,
Trying to keep my trotters warm."

Then suddenly, at his very feet, a cave opened in the silver sand and out came a tall woman wearing a dress of seaweed and shells, with ropes of pearls around her neck and a wonderful magical cap made of crayfish shell. All Jack could do was to stare in admiration and say:

"What a fine figure of a woman my eyes do now behold!"

"You may well say so," she replied. "My name is Jones, Miss Emily Jones, one of the famous submarine family of Davy Jones, who has a well-known locker. And who are you, Sailor Jack, and what are you doing on my island?"

"Ma'am," said Jack, "I was marooned here by pirates, something for which I'm very sorry. But having met you, why it becomes a pleasure and a privilege to be marooned on your floating island."

"Nicely put!" said Emily Jones, bowing like a sea wave, "but why did they maroon you?"

So Jack told her the whole story, while the moon rose higher and the monkeys crept around to listen too.

At the end of the tale Emily Jones sighed and said sadly, "Indeed, Jack, I feel for you something tremendous. I have often thought I'd like twenty boys myself."

Then Jack looked at the moon and thought he saw it wink at him. Speaking out boldly, as you'd expect such a sailor to speak, he said, "Madam, let's adopt the twenty boys together, for since I began to tell you the tale, it has occurred to me that, as well as twenty sons, I'd like a wife. And it has also occurred to me that you are the lass I'd like to marry – if you would be willing to accept the hand of a simple sailor."

Emily Jones blushed in the moonlight and looked at her feet in their oyster-shell shoes.

"Why, Jack," she said, "to be brisk and seamanlike, as becomes a member of the Jones family, the answer's yes! for I never met a man, fresh or salt, that I liked better."

"Well, now," said Jack, "you've made me the happiest man on the seven seas! Now, let's think of how to get to the wharf and meet Tom and the other orphans so that we can adopt them, for there *they* are, and here *we* are, and we've got to get from here to there."

"As to that," said Emily, "it's as easy as sneezing, for this island is *more* than an island. It is a boat, too! I am the captain, the monkeys are the crew, and the parrot is a lookout. Moreover, Jack, you don't need to worry about money for I have a fortune in pearls from my pet

oysters.'' And she led him to a vine-covered shed full of gleaming pearls of all sizes.

Then said Jack, ''*You* are the brightest treasure of the island, my pretty catfish, but we shall have a use for those pearls. Get your clever and amusing monkeys to hoist the sail and ho! for the wharf and our twenty orphans.''

So that is what they did. They came home to the wharf just exactly a year after Sailor Jack had left it. There was Tom, waiting for Jack, and with him were his orphan friends (the whole nineteen of them) and the board of governors from Bartholomew's Institution. As Jack and Emily sailed up the harbor, all the big boats and all the little ones blew their whistles and sirens, while all the sailors danced hornpipes and sang sea chanties, for they knew it was no ordinary sailor who came into port on a floating island with monkeys for a crew.

''I knew you'd come,'' said Tom.

''Well, I won't say it wasn't a struggle to get here,'' said Jack, ''but here I am.''

Luckily one of the board of governors was a minister of the Church, so Jack and Emily got married straight away.

Then Sailor Jack and his bride gave the board of governors two barrels of pearls (one of white pearls and the other of pink), and they quickly adopted the twenty orphans. So now there was a family of twenty boys, a mother (Emily) and a father (Jack), all of them going to live on board the little floating island.

Of course the board of governors invited them to stay for dinner.

"Thank you kindly," Jack answered, "but me and my new wife, Emily, must get out on our honeymoon with our twenty boys. We're going to have adventures such as you have never dreamed of. Aren't we, Emily? Aren't we, Tom?"

"We are!" said Emily and Tom firmly.

And, "We are!" shouted all nineteen boys.

"Some might say this is the happy ending," said Jack, "but I say, brisk and seamanlike as is my nature, it is just the happy beginning."

Then the parrot shouted, "Hoist aloft the sails!" The monkeys began to climb the palm tree, and the island moved merrily out of the harbor into the sunset. The board of governors waved good-bye.

"Perhaps they will come back," they said.

But the floating island, Jack, Emily, and the boys never ever came back again, for they were bound for places of enchantment about which no ordinary tale dares tell.

TOM TIB GOES SHOPPING

Little Tom Tib could stand on his head and walk on his hands. He could whistle like a blackbird and swim like a fish. In fact there were lots of things he could do, but there was one thing he could not do, try as he might. He could not remember what his mother told him to buy at the shop.

She told him to get bread, and he came back with a yellow umbrella. She told him to get butter, and he came back with a sugar sack full of Easter eggs. She told him to get a bottle of vinegar, and he came home with a baby elephant.

"Where on earth did you get *that*?" his mother asked him, but Tom Tib could not remember.

That was the way with Tom Tib. He could remember his nine-times table, he could remember to wash his knees – a thing a lot of boys forget to do – but he could not remember what he was supposed to buy at the shop.

"Tom Tib, Tom Tib," said his mother. "What can I do with a baby elephant? I won't send you to the shop ever again."

"Let me try once more," Tom Tib begged, and he begged and pleaded and wheedled so hard that his mother finally said,

"Very well, you can try once more, but this is your last chance. I would like you to get me a pot of honey. Now, so that you will remember, I will tell you this little rhyme:

Isn't it sticky, isn't it sweet? Just what a big bear loves to eat."

Tom Tib said the rhyme over and over to himself until he knew it by heart. Then he went off to the shop singing as he went.

Now, as it happened, on his way to the shop he met with a really, truly big bear. This big bear was in sad

trouble. He had stolen a tin can from somebody's shed, thinking it might have honey in it. He had opened the can and pushed his nose into it. Alas, the can was full of paint. The bear got paint in his eyes and mouth, and the can stuck on his nose and wouldn't come off.

As the bear was struggling with the can, Tom Tib went by, singing his rhyme:

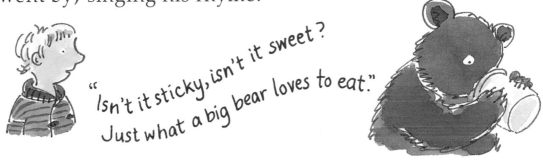

"Isn't it sticky, isn't it sweet? Just what a big bear loves to eat."

This made the bear so cross that he jerked with his paws, and the can flew off.

"Foolish boy!" snarled the bear. "You should say:

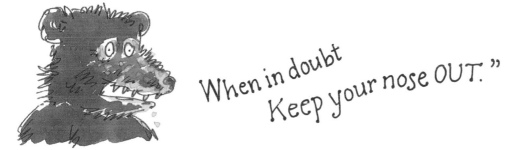

When in doubt Keep your nose OUT."

Now, the next person Tom Tibb met was a rose grower, a man who loved growing roses. He had just grown the loveliest red rose you ever saw. He was so excited that when he saw Tom Tib coming down the road he called, "Look at my rose. I say, look at my rose! Come here and I'll let you smell it, little lad."

But Tom Tib was busy trying to remember what it was he had to get at the shop, and he pranced along singing:

"When in doubt
Keep your nose OUT."

The rose grower was dreadfully annoyed. "Rude boy!" he screamed. "Listen! If somebody asks you to admire his beautiful red rose you should say:

What a truly wonderful smell, and
What a lovely red as well."

Immediately, Tom Tib forgot the bear's rhyme. He went on dancing along the road singing the words that the rose grower had told him to say.

Around the corner he came on a very strange sight indeed. Old Mr. Finn had thrown his rubbish out over the hedge. He did not look to see if anyone was passing by, and the rubbish had gone all over Mrs. Fat in her new silk dress and her straw hat.

Poor Mrs. Fat, all dirty and gray with dust. She had eggshells and fish bones in her hair, and she smelled of fish, too. Just then Tom Tib danced by singing:

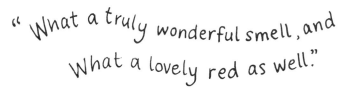

" What a truly wonderful smell, and what a lovely red as well."

Mrs. Fat hit Tom Tib with her umbrella.

"Are you making fun of me, Tom Tib?" she cried. "I'll skin you, I'll boil you, I'll bake you in butter! What you ought to say is:

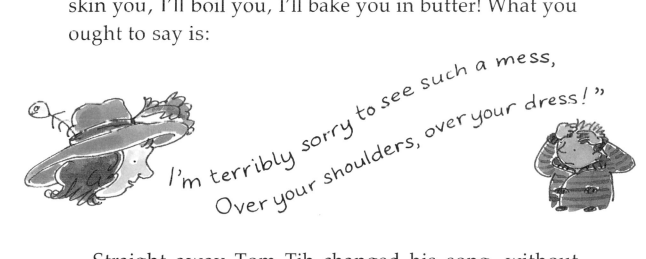

I'm terribly sorry to see such a mess, Over your shoulders, over your dress! "

Straight away Tom Tib changed his song, without really knowing that he had changed it. Off he went and at last he came to the shop. There, on a stool by the shop door sat Daffodil, the shopkeeper's daughter, combing her golden hair. And beside her was Nobby the carpenter, nailing up a new step for the shop.

Up came Tom Tib, cheerful as a cricket, and, taking one look at Daffodil's long and tumbling golden hair, he sang:

"I'm terribly sorry to see such a mess, Over your shoulders, over your dress."

Nobby the carpenter looked up from his work.

"Tom Tib," he said, "you'll never get far if you say things like that to a pretty girl combing her hair. What you should say is:

"Sweetest gold from here to home Keep it nice and use a comb."

That was enough for Tom Tib. He forgot Mrs. Fat's words and could remember only Nobby's.

"Now, Tom Tib," said the shopkeeper, "what is it you want today? We're out of elephants, you know."

"Oh, it's not an elephant," Tom Tib said. "At least I don't *think* so. I can't quite remember. But my mother told me a rhyme to help me remember it. Listen!

Sweetest gold from here to home,
Keep it nice and use a comb."

"Why," said the shopkeeper, "*that's* easy! Your mother wants a pot of honey."

"So she does!" said Tom Tib. "I remembered the rhyme, didn't I?"

Tom Tib's mother was delighted when he turned up with the honey.

"Well, you must be improving," she said. "How clever of you to remember my rhyme all the way to the shop!"

"Perhaps I *was* a bit clever," said Tom Tib, looking pleased.

But who do *you* think was the clever one?

CAT AND MOUSE

One summer's day, a young mouse set out looking for adventure.

"Be very careful!" said his mother. "It's a dangerous world for mice. Watch out for traps, and watch out for the sharp claws of the cat, and, above all, don't be too sure of anything."

As the mouse ran in and out of the stems of the sunflowers, a cat saw him and called out in a sweet voice, "Hello there, Mouse!"

The mouse stopped, hearing his name called, and looked out nervously.

"Come on out, Mouse, and talk to me," the cat said. "I'm rather lonely, and I'd love a bit of company."

"But aren't you a cat?" asked the young and innocent mouse.

"A cat? Perish the thought!" cried the cat piously. "I am none other than Santa Claus. Look at my white whiskers and white eyebrows if you don't believe me."

The mouse had heard that Santa Claus had white whiskers and white eyebrows, and also that he gave people presents.

"Are you absolutely *sure* you're Santa Claus?" he asked, because there was still something about the cat that made him very suspicious.

"Of course I am," said the cat. "Look! Here are my claws to prove it. That's why I'm called Santa Claus. Come on out. I have presents and things for you just down the path."

As the mouse came out from among the sunflower stems, the cat pounced on him, catching him straight away.

"You should never believe everything you hear," the cat said, "because now I am going to eat you up."

"You said we'd talk together," cried the terrified mouse, realizing he had been tricked.

"Well, we'll talk a bit first if you like," said the cat. "And then I'll eat you up afterward. I have plenty of time, and I'm not terribly hungry. I just liked the thought of catching a mouse."

The mouse thought very quickly.

"What makes you sure I am a mouse?" he asked. "You're not very clever for a cat."

"Well, you *are* a mouse," said the cat.

The mouse made himself laugh very hard. He didn't feel much like laughing. He just made himself laugh through sheer willpower.

"I'm not a mouse," he said, when he had finished laughing, "I'm a dog."

It was the cat's turn to laugh, but it was a very surprised laugh. He had never caught a mouse like this one before.

"I know a mouse when I see one."

"No – I'm definitely a dog!" declared the mouse, still laughing, "and when I get my breath back, I'm going to bark at you and chase you up a tree."

Inside his mouse mind he was telling himself: I'm not a mouse . . . I'm a dog. I'm *not* a mouse. I'm a *dog*. He made himself think dog thoughts.

"Just imagine you thinking that I am a mouse!" he cried.

"Well, you look *quite* like a mouse," the cat said, sounding rather less sure of himself. The mouse was looking a lot more like a dog than the cat had thought at first.

"Let me hear you bark!" the cat commanded.

"Wait a moment . . ." In his mouse mind he was telling himself: Think *dog*! Bark *dog*! Be *dog*! "Well, are you ready?"

"Yes!" said the cat.

"Then stand back a bit because I don't want to deafen you with my barking," the mouse said, and the cat actually did stand back a bit, though he kept one paw firmly on the mouse's tail. The mouse barked as well as he could, but it came out very like a mouse's squeak.

"There!" said the cat triumphantly, "and I'm going to eat you straight away because I can see you're a very tricky mouse."

The mouse did not lose his head, even though he thought the cat might take it off with a single bite.

"You really do have mice on the brain. It'll serve you right when I chase you up a tree."

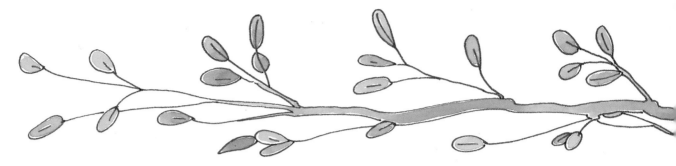

"Think *dog*! Be *dog*!" he muttered under his whiskers. He made himself laugh in an easygoing fashion.

As he spoke, a strange thing happened to the mouse. By now he believed he actually *was* a dog. The cat, which had looked so terrible a moment ago, began to look small and silly. Cowardly, too! He felt *dogness* swell up inside him. He thought he could remember burying bones, fighting other dogs, and, of course, chasing many, many cats. He felt a bark swelling in his throat. He barked again.

My goodness! the cat thought. He really *is* a dog, and here I am with my paw on his tail. The cat looked nervous and the mouse felt very strong. He opened his

mouth and barked for a third time. This time there was no doubt about it: It was a really wonderful bark. The cat took his paw off the mouse's tail and ran for the tree with the mouse chasing him, barking furiously. The cat shot up the tree like a furry rocket and hid among the leaves.

Whew! That was a narrow escape, thought the cat, cowering at the top of the tree.

Whew! That was a narrow escape, thought the mouse at the bottom of the tree. I'm off home to Mother!

As he reached the mousehole he saw his mother, nervously collecting sunflower seeds outside.

"Mother!" called the mouse. "Here I am, home again."

"Ahhhhh! A dog!" screamed his mother and popped down into the mousehole.

The mouse lay outside in the sun with his paws stretched in front of him and his tongue hanging out.

"Think *mouse*," he panted. "Think *mouse*!"

So he thought *mouse* and, as he thought *mouse*, the *dogness* died away.

"What am I doing sitting out here in broad daylight with my tongue hanging out?" he squeaked to himself. "I must be mad. That cat could come back at any moment."

Then he scuttled into the mousehole where his mother met him with great delight.

"I'm glad you're back," she said. "It's dangerous out there. A big dog ran at me, barking."

"A cat caught me," the mouse said, "but I escaped."

"Escaped? Oh, my son! How did you manage that?"

"Cleverness," said the mouse modestly. "Cleverness and courage. I chased the cat up the tree."

Exaggerating again, thought his mother, fondly.

Then the mouse and his mother had a delicious dinner of sunflower seeds.

As for the cat, he stayed up in the tree all day for fear of the savage dog that was waiting somewhere below in the summer garden.

eight

THE KING'S TOYS

When the king was just a little king, his mother, who was very strict, would not let him have any toys at all.

"You are a king," she said. "You must take life seriously. You must learn to spell."

His mother, the queen, thought that knowing how to spell was most important for a king. She had a room specially designed for him in which to practice his spelling.

When he was nearly a grown-up king, his mother left for a few days to visit her aunt who lived on top of a glass mountain. While his mother was away, the king decided to give himself a treat: He would buy a toy. By now he was the best speller of any monarch in the world, but in his entire life he had never had a single toy.

Summoning the royal librarian, the king asked him: "Librarians are meant to know everything. What toy would you suggest I buy?"

"Well, when I was small," said the librarian, "I used to be very fond of my teddy bear."

"Right!" said the king. So he sent his butler out to buy a teddy bear.

But the butler, who did not wish to be seen buying a toy, sent for a footman and told him to go instead.

But the footman did not want to be seen buying a teddy bear. So he sent for the page boy and told him to go in his place.

But the page boy, who was almost thirteen and very grown-up, did not want anyone to see him buying a teddy bear either. So he sent for the kitchen boy, Jack – the youngest of the king's staff.

Jack could scarcely believe his luck. He ran to the toy shop across the road from the palace and bought a beautiful, large, golden teddy bear. He gave it to the page boy, who gave it to the footman, who gave it to the butler, who gave it to the king.

The king sat the bear on the mantelpiece in the royal spelling room.

"I like this bear," he said. "I like it so much that perhaps I should get another one. It will be rather lonely by itself."

"Why not try a rocking horse next?" suggested the librarian.

The king sent for the butler, who sent for the footman, who sent for the page boy, who sent for Jack. Jack chose a wonderful dapple-gray rocking horse with a long mane, an even longer tail, and a bridle hung all over with golden bells.

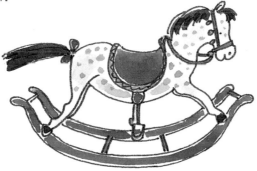

Now that the king had a teddy bear and a rocking horse, there was no stopping him. Jack was busy all day running across the road to the toy shop, and then dashing back again with big packages tied with shiny ribbon. Every day was like Christmas for the king.

Jack chose a Noah's ark for him,

and then a monkey on a stick,

and a dollhouse –
with tiny plants,
a rocking chair, a pink cake
on the kitchen table, as well
as a dear little four-poster bed.

Jack bought a windup clown,
building blocks,

and a tin man in a checked coat
who went *wibble-wobble*,
wibble-wobble up and
down a tin ladder.

He chose hero dolls
with bulging muscles,

and robot dolls that obeyed orders, an electric train,

and four racing cars.

The king's royal spelling room gradually became a
royal toy room. Soon it was so full of toys that there
wasn't room for any more.

"Right!" exclaimed the king. "That's enough. Now
let's see what happens next."

Sending for his golden throne (which two footmen trundled along the palace corridors to the royal spelling room), the king sat down. He looked at his huge collection of toys, waiting for them to do something. He sat there, on and off, for three days – waiting expectantly. The teddy bear stared back at him, and so did the rocking horse. The dolls in the dollhouse, the hero dolls, the robot dolls, and the tin man in the checked coat all stared at the king, and he stared back at them. Nobody did anything. At last, the king sent for the butler.

"I certainly have a lot of toys," he said.

"You do have a lovely collection, Your Majesty," agreed the butler.

"Yes, but when are they going to *do* something?" the king asked.

But the butler seemed to have forgotten exactly what toys were supposed to do.

"One moment," he said, and shot off through the maze of palace corridors to find the footman. "Just remind me," the butler said, "for it's a long time since I had any toys myself . . . what are the king's toys supposed to *do*?"

"Just remind me," the footman said, hurrying to the page boy. "What are those toys supposed to *do*?"

The page boy ran to the kitchen and found Jack scrubbing soup off a royal saucepan.

"The king has been waiting for his toys to *do* something," he cried. "They won't budge!"

"Why not let me talk to the king?" Jack suggested boldly. So the page boy took Jack to the footman, and the footman took him to the butler, and the butler took him to the king.

"His Majesty wishes to know when the toys are going to *do* something," the butler said sternly to Jack. Jack looked at the king. He looked at the toys.

"Your Majesty, *you* are the one who has to do something," Jack cried. "Toys are meant to be *played* with. They are waiting for you to *play* with them."

"Play?" cried the king. He spelled the word. "P-L-A-Y! But how do I P-L-A-Y?"

"I'll show you!" cried Jack. Grabbing the teddy bear, he leaped on to the rocking horse. Then he rocked until the horse nearly came off its elegant rockers. He made the dollhouse dolls ask the hero dolls and robot dolls to tea, and they all had a slice of pink cake, and yet there was plenty left over.

"I'm beginning to get the idea," said the king excitedly, seizing a green racing car. He put one of the hero dolls in the driving seat and set it off *brrroom*, *brrrooming* around the room, making tooting noises at every corner.

When the king's mother came back from her visit to the glass mountain, she realized her son would never be the same again. The king had appointed Jack his minister of play, and they played with the toys together every day – to keep in practice. And in return, the king taught Jack how to S-P-E-L-L, and even to R-E-A-D, and what could have been fairer than that?

THE STRANGE EGG

Once, Molly found a strange leathery egg in the swamp. She put it under Mrs. Warm, the broody hen, to hatch it out. It hatched out into a sort of dragon.

Her father said, "This is no ordinary dragon. This is a dinosaur."

"What is a dinosaur?" asked Molly.

"Well," said her father, "a long time ago there were a lot of dinosaurs. They were all big lizards. Some of them were bigger than houses. They all died long ago. All except this one," he added gloomily. "I hope it is not one of the larger meat-eating lizards as then it might grow up to worry the sheep."

The dinosaur followed Mrs. Warm about. She scratched worms for it, but the dinosaur liked plants better.

"Ah," said Molly's father. "It is a plant-eating dinosaur – one of the milder kind. They are stupid but good-natured," he added.

Professors of all ages came from near and far to see Molly's dinosaur. She led it around on a string. Every day she needed a longer piece of string. The dinosaur grew as big as ten elephants. It ate all the flowers in the garden, and Molly's mother got cross.

"I am tired of having no garden and I am tired of making tea for all the professors," she said. "Let's send the dinosaur to the zoo."

"No," said Father. "The place wouldn't be the same without it."

So the dinosaur stayed. Mrs. Warm used to perch on it every night. She had never before hatched such a grand, successful egg.

One day it began to rain. . . . It rained and rained and rained and rained so heavily that the water in the river was soon so deep it overflowed.

"A flood, a flood – we will drown," screamed Molly's mother.

"Hush, dear," said Molly's father. "We will ride to a safe place on Molly's dinosaur. Whistle to it, Molly."

Molly whistled and the dinosaur came toward her with Mrs. Warm the hen, wet and miserable, on its back. Molly and her father and mother climbed onto the dinosaur's back with her. They held an umbrella over themselves and had warm drinks out of a thermos flask. Just as they left, the house was swept away by the flood.

"Well, dear, there you are," said Molly's father. "You see it was useful to have a dinosaur, after all. And I am now able to tell you that this is the biggest kind of dinosaur and its name is *Diplodocus*."

Molly was pleased to think her pet had such a long, dignified-sounding name. It matched it well. As they went along, they rescued a lot of other people climbing trees and housetops, and floating on chicken crates and fruit boxes. They rescued cats and dogs, two horses, and an elephant that was floating away from a circus. The dinosaur paddled on cheerfully. By the time they came in sight of dry land, its back was quite crowded. On the land police officers were getting boats ready to go looking for people, but all the people were safe on the dinosaur's back.

After the flood went down and everything was as it should be, a fine medal was awarded to Molly's dinosaur as Most Heroic Animal of the Year, and many presents were given to it.

The biggest present of all was a great big swimming pool made of rubber so it could be blown up. It was so big it took one man nearly a year to blow it up. It was a good size for dinosaurs of the *Diplodocus* type. It lived in the swimming pool after that (and Molly's mother was able to grow her flowers again). It is well known that diplodocuses like to swim and paddle. It took the weight off its feet. Mrs. Warm the hen used to swim with it a bit, and it is not very often you find a swimming hen.

So you see this story has a happy ending after all, which is not easy with a pet as big as ten elephants. And just to end the story I must tell you that though Molly's dinosaur had the long name of *Diplodocus*, Molly always called it Rosie.

THE BOY WHO BOUNCED

Once there was a little boy who had a very bad habit indeed. He used to bounce like a ball.

Wherever he went his mother would say: "Walk like a little gentleman." But he wouldn't. He bounced instead.

His father said: "No one in our family has ever bounced before. I wish you would do something else. You could run a bit, or even hop, or you could skip."

The little boy took no notice at all. This was a mistake because one day he bounced on a magician who was snoozing in the sun. The magician was very cross.

"It is really too much," he cried. "I came out for a quiet day in the country and what happens? First I'm chased by a bull (I had to turn it into a canary-bird to get away). Then I'm chased by the farmer who owned the bull (I had to change a foxglove into a lot of money to pay him). It has left me very tired. I lie down to have a snooze and a nasty little boy comes and bounces on me. Pah! Say you're sorry, little boy, and walk off quietly."

The rude little boy took no notice of the magician. He started to bounce away. The magician became very angry indeed.

"If you want to bounce, well—bounce you shall," he declared, and began to mutter magic words very quickly. The little boy felt suddenly strange around his fingers and toes – a sort of pins-and-needles feeling. (That was the magic working.) Before he could say "Mousetrap!" he had turned into a red rubber ball – a big ball, a bouncing ball. He could bounce so softly that he wouldn't break a cobweb if he bounced on it. He could bounce as high as a pine tree.

"Meet me here in a year's time," the magician said, "and I'll think about whether or not to turn you into a boy again." Then he lay down and began to snooze once more.

The Bouncer leaped over the creek and began to go around the world. He felt quite happy because now he could bounce so much better than before. As he went past the school all the children came running out trying to catch him, but he went too fast for them. Soon he reached the sea.

He couldn't bounce very easily on the water. Instead the waves helped him along. They were delighted to have such a fine red ball to play with and they tossed him to one another until he reached Africa.

Lions opened their yellow eyes as the Bouncer went past and the giraffes stretched their necks to see him. They stretched them so far that all the giraffes in that part of Africa have longer necks than any other giraffes, which makes them very proud and conceited.

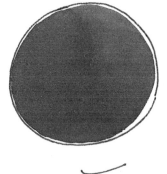

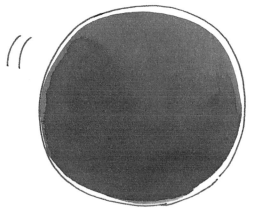

He went through all sorts of countries with names I can't spell, and his fine red paint wore off so he became a gray, battered-looking bouncer. He went more slowly now and had to stop to catch his breath. When he stopped, he hid. It was one day while he was hiding that he overheard two men talking.

"I hear they have caught a wicked magician," the first man said.

"Well, I don't know if he is wicked or not," the second man said in reply, "but they are going to beat him. Would you like to come and watch?"

"Yes I would," said the first man.

How unfair! the Bouncer thought. Poor magician! I shall rescue him!

He followed the men, bouncing so softly they did not hear him.

The magician was brought out from prison, and twelve men in black stood with sticks to beat him. He looked small and old and his gingery whiskers drooped sadly. That isn't my magician, the Bouncer thought, but he is very like him.

Then, just as the twelve men were lifting their sticks to beat the magician, the Bouncer gave a tremendous *bounce* and knocked them all head over heels. Quick as a cat the magician leaped onto the Bouncer's back and off they went on great, high bounces as high as the trees.

"Turn to the left," the magician whispered. "Then go over the river and turn to the right. We will be in another country after that and we will find my brother snoozing beside a creek."

So the Bouncer did as he was told and, sure enough, it wasn't long before he recognized his home and the creek where he had bounced on the first magician. There the first magician was – still snoozing, with grass growing over him, looking like an old mossy log. He sat up, rubbing his eyes, as the Bouncer came along.

"What! You back so soon?" he said.

"You said to come back in a year," the Bouncer replied, "and I would like a change from bouncing."

"He has been very good!" said the second magician. "He saved me when they were going to beat me."

"Oh well," said the first magician, "I suppose you can be a boy again, but you've got to walk from now on, not bounce."

He muttered his magic words backward and there was the boy again, only his clothes were too small for him now because he was a year taller.

He thanked the magicians, and they went one way and he the other – all the way back home. His mother frowned at him when he came in.

"You're late!" she said. "Your dinner got cold and we had to give it to the cat."

"I've been bouncing around the world," said the boy. "It's made me pretty hungry."

"I'll make you a sandwich," she said, with a laugh, "but you mustn't ever be so late again."

And that is the story of the boy who was turned into a Bouncer. He was always very careful when he walked about after that, in case he bounced on a magician.

THE KINGS OF THE
BROOM CUPBOARD

Once there was a family who moved to a new house. It was just a small family – a mother, a father, and a little girl called Sarah. Well, this house was not exactly new – in fact it was one of those big old houses full of space and echoes. Footsteps sounded loud and doors shut like guns going off. The family were a bit nervous of this different house, and felt it was always watching them, waiting to surprise them. Some of the furniture had already been put inside the house, and some was still on its way in the van. The furniture in the house looked nervous, too – as if in this new house, no one would dust it or sweep beneath it.

Her mother was making lunch when Sarah came and said, "Mommy, you know that big cupboard in the hall?"

"Yes," said her mother, "that's a broom cupboard."

"Well, there's a king in it, Mommy. He's been shut in there for years and years."

"That's a pity," said her mother. "Why doesn't he come out?"

"He can't!" said Sarah. "He's enchanted. Spiders have spun all over him, Mommy."

"Poor king!" said her mother.

"Poor king!" repeated Sarah. Then she thought for a while and said, "Why don't you rescue him, Mommy?"

"I promise I would if I knew how to do it," her mother replied.

"I'll go and ask how," said Sarah, and off she went.

Her mother finished the sandwiches and cut some cake before Sarah came back.

"You've just got to unlock the door and the king and his friends will come out," she told her mother.

"What? Is it locked?" asked her mother, surprised. "Then how do you know there's a king in there?"

"I heard him whispering to be let out," Sarah said. "There's a draft under the broom cupboard door and that king has a sore throat. He's had it for years. He can only whisper and rustle. I tried to look through the keyhole, but it was too dark to see anything."

"All joking aside," said her mother, who did not believe in the king for one whispering, rustling moment, "I wonder if we have the key for that door." She took up a key ring from the table and started looking at the keys. "This is for the back door, this is for the front door, this is for the study at the end of the hall."

"A witch enchanted the king," Sarah told her mother. "The king and his friends were having a picnic when, for no reason at all, this witch enchanted them.

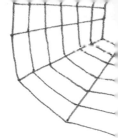

Then she built a cupboard around them. Then she built a house around the cupboard – this house. That's how it got here. And then that witch just stood there, laughing in a nasty way. Have you found the key?''

''No, there doesn't seem to be any key here,'' said her mother.

Sarah looked worried.

''There should be!'' she cried.  ''The king says today is the day he is to come out.''

''He'll have to wait until I find the key,'' said her mother.

But at that moment a blue pigeon flew into the room. It settled on the table and dropped a tiny black key onto her mother's bread-and-butter plate. Then it cooed in a conceited fashion and did a conceited dance, before it flew out of the window again.

''I told you!'' Sarah cried. ''It's all working out. That's the key!''

''Well, what a thing to happen!'' said her mother. ''I wonder if it is the key to the broom cupboard?'' And she went into the hall to find out. Sarah ran with her.

As her mother jiggled the key in the lock, Sarah called encouragingly, ''Are you there, King? Are you listening? It won't be a moment now.''

''I'm afraid the keyhole has rusted up,'' said her mother sadly. ''The king will have to wait.''

But at that very moment there came a small clinking

and clanking, and four mice came down the hall dragging an oilcan. They dropped it at Sarah's feet and ran back to their holes.

"That's useful," said her mother, though she was frowning a bit at the thought of mice in the house. She picked up the oilcan and oiled, first the key and then the keyhole.

The key turned easily.

Out from the cupboard came a light like sunshine, the smell of flowers and tomato sandwiches, and the sound of drums and trumpets. Out came not one, but seven kings and four queens wearing robes of purple and gold. Out came a whole procession of dancing people dressed in green with flowers in their hair. Out came a whole herd of silver deer, strutting peacocks, and a pink elephant with a rose tied to its tail.

Last of all came a witch, dragging a broom after her. She looked crossly at Sarah and her mother.

"I enchanted myself into that broom cupboard by accident," she muttered. "A wrong word in the wrong place . . ."

The kings and the queens, the people in green, the silver deer, the strutting peacocks, and the pink elephant went down the hall in a sort of parade and a sort of dance. They went one step grave and one step gay, out into the lovely summer day, off through the overgrown garden and then into the trees. Their colors shone, flashed, and were lost.

The witch threw the broom back into the cupboard.

"Get in there where you belong!" she snarled. "No more enchanting for me. I've had a change of heart." She called to the kings, "Wait for me!" Then she went scuttling after them like a mud-colored mouse.

Sarah's mother stared in amazement. After a moment she opened the door of the broom cupboard and peered inside uncertainly.

"There's just that broom left," she said. But the broom hopped out on its stumpy, bumpy handle, right down the hall, across the garden and into the wood, chasing after the witch and the kings.

"Now it's empty," Sarah said with a sigh of satisfaction. "There's room for our own brooms. They should be happy there – it's a nice cupboard. It's good when enchantments work out properly and there's a happy ending."

From somewhere outside came the echoes of trumpets and drums as the kings of the broom cupboard went on their way.

THE TICK TOCK PARTY

One day Timothy said to his mother, "It is a long time since Christmas. And we haven't had a party for ages. Will it be my birthday soon?"

"Not for another long time!" his mother said. "We are just halfway between Christmastime and birthday time."

"Couldn't we have my birthday a bit sooner this year?" asked Timothy.

"Not really!" said his mother. "It is best to have your birthday when it comes."

Timothy looked around sadly. Out in the yard he saw Tick Tock the old gray rocking horse.

"Couldn't it be Tick Tock's birthday then?" he asked. "Tick Tock is so old his birthday cake would be like a bonfire with all its candles. Let it be his birthday."

Mother thought for a while.

"Yes," she said, "Tick Tock deserves a birthday. He is very old indeed. First he was Granny's rocking horse, then he was mine. Now he is yours. His mane has come off and his tail is lost. All his fine paint is gone. He must feel very old and gray. We will have a party on Saturday to cheer him up."

Timothy ran out into the yard to tell Tick Tock.

"It is your birthday on Saturday, Tick Tock," he said. "Isn't that exciting? Aren't you pleased?"

But Tick Tock just looked as sad and gray as ever. Timothy was the one to be excited. Thursday went by, and then Friday. At last it was Saturday – the day of the birthday. It was a beautiful sunny morning. Timothy woke up and the first thing he did was to run outside, pajamas and all, to say happy birthday to Tick Tock. He ran into the sunny yard, and stopped in surprise. Tick Tock was not gray anymore. He was shining white all over.

Mother and Father laughed at Timothy's surprise.

"This is part of my birthday present to Tick Tock," Father said. "I will give him the rest of his present this afternoon when the white paint is quite dry."

Timothy was very pleased to think that Tick Tock had been given a birthday present.

All morning he played in the yard. He could not keep his eyes off the shining white shape of Tick Tock.

Just before lunch a car pulled up at the gate.

"Mommy!" called Timothy. "Here are Granny and Grandpa!"

"We couldn't miss Tick Tock's birthday," Granny said. "I have a present for him."

Tick Tock couldn't unwrap his present, so Timothy had to unwrap it for him. Granny had made a fine red saddle with golden tassels. Grandpa had a package, too. At first Timothy could not think what it was. It seemed to be filled with long black hair.

"It is a new tail for Tick Tock made of real horse-hair," said Grandpa. "Your father will nail it on for him – and the saddle, too – when the paint is dry."

So now Tick Tock had a new white coat, a red saddle, and a black tail.

Someone opened the gate. It was Aunt Joan.

"I had to come to Tick Tock's party," she said. "Here is his present."

Timothy unwrapped the package. It was full of brown sheep's wool.

"It is from a special brown sheep I know," said Aunt Joan. "It is a mane for Tick Tock, but I see you will have to wait before we put it on."

So now Tick Tock had a fine brown mane to toss in the wind.

"It does not match his tail," said Timothy, "but that is all the better."

Then Anne, Timothy's big sister, came out into the yard to join them.

"Look," she said, "I have a present for Tick Tock, too. It is a red bridle. I made it all myself."

"Thank you," said Timothy, because Tick Tock was too busy thinking about his presents to say thank you for himself.

"Well, this is all very well," said Timothy's mother, "but *my* present to Tick Tock is waiting inside. Let's go in and look at it."

Inside, the table was set for lunch, and in the middle of the table was a big birthday cake with more candles on it than Timothy had ever seen. Everyone laughed and talked and ate birthday cake.

It was a wonderful party. Outside, Tick Tock stood like a ghost horse, white and shining in the sunlight.

"Ah," said Granny, "I remember the morning when I first saw Tick Tock. It was Christmas, and I was only a little girl then. He was the most wonderful Christmas present I had ever had. He was dapple gray in those days with a long white mane and tail."

"Then, when I was small," said Aunt Joan, "Father – that's Grandpa to you, Timothy – brought him down from the attic and painted him up again."

"Aunt Joan and I used to play on him for hours at a time," said Mother. "We'd ride him together, or pretend he was a wild horse we were trying to catch and tame. Whenever I felt sad I would go and sit on Tick Tock and rock and rock until I felt better."

"And now he's mine," said Timothy proudly.

"Quite a member of the family in fact," said Father. "I think the paint is dry enough now. We'll give Tick Tock a really new look for his birthday."

They all went out and watched Father nail on the black tail and tack on the brown mane. He fitted the saddle and bridle on and fastened them with little nails. Last of all he took a pot of blue paint, and with a small paintbrush he painted two beautiful blue eyes for Tick Tock to see with.

"Good old Tick Tock," said Anne. "He looks like new."

"He's smiling at me," Timothy cried.

"So he should be, with all those presents," said Father, laughing. He lifted Timothy onto the new red saddle. "You give him a birthday present now, Timothy," Father said. "Take him for a good rocky ride."

So Timothy rocked away, and Tick Tock's rockers went "Tick Tock!" on the ground, which was, no doubt, his rocking horse way of saying "Thank you."